HiDiNG PHiL

by Eric Barclay

Scholastic Press • New York

For Michelle, Emma, and Paige

I would like to thank David Saylor and Orli Zuravicky for lending me their expertise and providing gracious direction along the way.

Thank you to Kirsten Hall for helping Phil find an exceptionally good home.

To my good friend Vanessa Brantley Newton: Thank you for always being there with a quick laugh and an honest critique.

Library of Congress Cataloging-in-Publication Data
Barclay, Eric. • Hiding Phil / story & pictures by Eric Barclay. — 1st ed.   p. cm.
Summary: Three siblings come upon an elephant named Phil and decide to bring him home—and then they have to hide him from their parents.
ISBN 978-0-545-46477-2 (HC) / ISBN 978-0-545-60456-7 (POB)
1. Elephants—Juvenile fiction. 2. Brothers and sisters—Juvenile fiction.
[1. Elephants—Fiction. 2. Brothers and sisters—Fiction.] I. Title.
PZ7.B2357Hid 2013 • 813.6—dc23 • 2012049321

10 9 8 7 6 5 4 3 2 1   13 14 15 16 17

Printed in China   38
First edition, September 2013
Book design by Eric Barclay and Chelsea C. Donaldson

Whee!

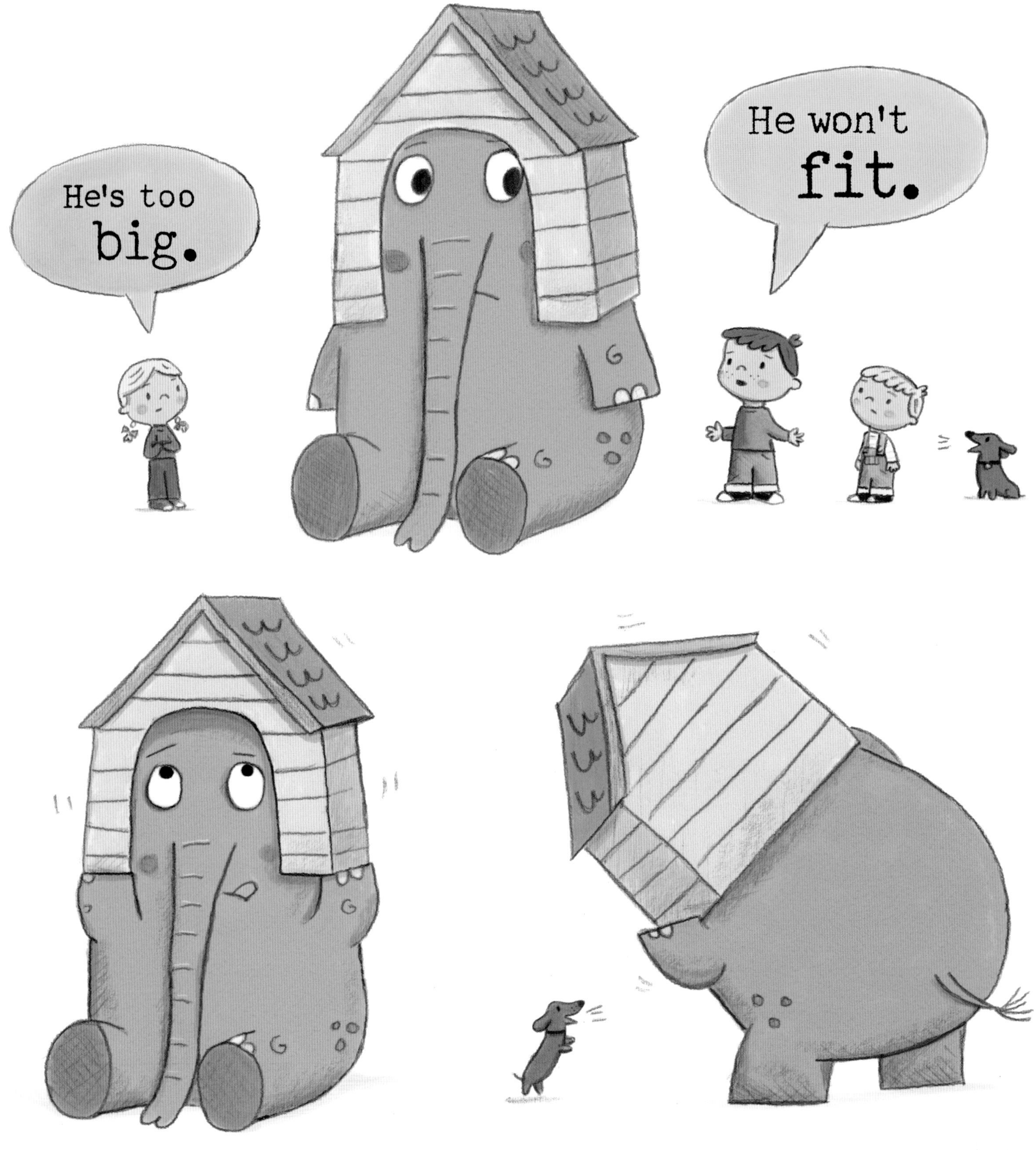
He's too big.
He won't fit.